MERRYLEGS

PAM SMY

Magic happens in the hush of the night
when the stars start to glitter
and the moon shines bright.

Poor old Merrylegs.

Stumble clump
clippetty clomp
clump, clomp, clump

With his head down and his eyes on the ground,
Merrylegs plodded and clomped.
Round and round, day after day,
teaching the children how to ride.

And because he never lifted his head
he never saw the children on his back.
He just **plodded** and **clomped**
around the stables and wished his life
was more exciting.

Stumble clump
clippetty clomp
clump, clomp, clump

Each evening, Merrylegs and his friend, Feathers, watched the racehorses dashing by.

"How happy those riders must be," sighed Merrylegs. "Oh, I wish I was as tall and beautiful as those horses."

MERRYLEGS

For Alice Corrie

with thanks

"You should see how happy the children are to ride you!" chirped Feathers.

But Merrylegs wasn't listening.

One summer evening, Feathers flew across
the yard and settled on Merrylegs' stable door.
"The fair is in town,
the fair is in town!
Let's go!"

So off they went.

The friends looked down at the fair.
Merrylegs couldn't believe his eyes!
He was mesmerized.

There were stalls, tents and hot-dog
stands. Children bustled and ran
carrying candyfloss, balloons and
coins. The air was full of music
and laughter.

And in the middle of it all . . .

a carousel.

Merrylegs had never seen
such beautiful horses. Their eyes
flashed. Their manes flowed.
And their painted bodies
glowed scarlet and gold.
As they spun round, the
children laughed and waved.

"Look how happy the
children are on those
beautiful horses,"
sighed Merrylegs.

"That's *just* how they look riding on *your* back!" insisted Feathers.

But Merrylegs wasn't listening.

He just wished and watched and watched and wished until evening came, the children left, and the fair became still.

Night fell.

In the moonlight,
Merrylegs squeezed through
the hedge into the fairground.
He trotted up to
the carousel.

Lifting his head
and pointing his hooves
like the shining horses,
Merrylegs trotted round and round.

He stretched out his legs
and swished his tail.
Round and round. Faster and faster.

"It's no use!" cried Merrylegs, exhausted. "I am *not* a racehorse, *or* a carousel horse. I am *not* tall *or* beautiful. I am just a stumbling, plodding riding school pony."

Wearily, Merrylegs plodded back to his paddock.
As he hung his sleepy head, all he could hear was,

Stumble clump
  clippetty clomp
  clump, clomp, clump

Merrylegs fell asleep.

Magic happens in the
hush of the night
when the stars start to glitter
and the moon
shines bright.

When he opened

his eyes . . .

He saw a carousel horse –
bright-eyed with shining paint,
rippling mane and
swishing tail.

As Merrylegs looked on, the carousel
horse stretched his legs, whipped
his tail, jumped out of the fairground
and into the moonlight beyond.

"Go!" chirped
Feathers.

And Merrylegs did.

The horses raced through the town.

Together they leapt walls
and galloped over fields.

Into the woods they chased,
faster and faster,
up onto the hill
above.

And at the crest of the hill
they stopped.

Merrylegs held his head
up high and gazed
at the sky.

His nostils **flared**,
his mane **flowed**
and his tail **swished**.

"Fly!" called Feathers.

Merrylegs took a breath . . .

. . . and together
they flew.

The next day the sun rose. The fairground had packed up and gone.
The children in the riding school waited for their lessons.

Everything was the same . . .

. . . except Merrylegs.

Snippetty trip,
clippetty trip,
trip, trot, trip

His tail swishes, his hooves lift and his head is held high. His pricked ears catch each giggle of delight from the children on his back.

And if you look closely, you can see that Merrylegs' eyes are full of dreams.

MERRYLEGS
is a
DAVID FICKLING BOOK

First published in Great Britain by
David Fickling Books,
31 Beaumont Street,
Oxford, OX1 2NP

www.davidficklingbooks.com

Hardback edition published 2019
This edition published 2020

Text and illustrations © Pam Smy

978-1-78845-058-4

1 3 5 7 9 10 8 6 4 2

WARNING: THIS BOOK WILL FILL YOUR EYES WITH DREAMS . . .

Papers used by David Fickling Books are from well-managed forests
and other responsible sources.

FSC
www.fsc.org
MIX
Paper from
responsible sources
FSC® C104723

DAVID FICKLING BOOKS Reg. No. 8340307

A CIP catalogue record for this book is available
from the British Library.

Printed and bound in China by Toppan Leefung

Edited by Alice Corrie
Designed by Ness Wood